PADDINGTON

STORYBOOK FAVORITES

PLEASE LOOK AFTER THIS BEAR. Thank you.

ISBN 978-0-06-297274-3

Typography by Lori S. Malkin

19 20 21 22 23   GPS   10 9 8 7 6 5 4 3 2   ❖   First Edition

Michael Bond
PADDINGTON
Storybook Favorites

illustrated by R. W. Alley

HARPER
An Imprint of HarperCollinsPublishers

CONTENTS

PADDINGTON
and the Busy Bee Carnival

ne day Paddington's friend Mr. Gruber took him on a surprise outing to a part of London known as "Little Venice."

"It's called Little Venice because it's by a canal," he explained, "and every Spring they hold a big Carnival. Boats come from all over the country to take part in the celebration."

Paddington always enjoyed his days out with Mr. Gruber. He waved as one of the boats went past. All the people on board waved back at him.

"I've never been for a ride on a canal before," said
Paddington.

"Who knows," said Mr. Gruber mysteriously,
"perhaps you will before the day is out. But first of all,
we must see what else is happening. We don't want to
miss anything important."

He pointed to a board showing all the different events, but there were so many Paddington didn't know which to try first. "How about the Busy Bee Adventure Trail?" suggested Mr. Gruber. "You have to find as many things as possible beginning with the letter B."

Paddington thought that sounded like a very good idea, especially when Mr. Gruber told him the first prize was a free boat ride for two.

"Bears are good at trails, Mr. Gruber," he explained.

Looking around he could already see lots of things beginning with the letter B. Apart from B for BOARD, there was a BOY blowing BUBBLES, a man eating a BAGEL and another with a BROOM, a BARBECUE, and a lady selling BANANAS. There were BOATS everywhere and lots of BALLOONS. There was even a man playing the BANJO in a BAND.

After Paddington had finished writing them all down, he and Mr. Gruber set off along the canal.

In no time at all, Paddington had added five other items to his list: first there was B for BRIDGE, and then BLACKBIRD, BUTTERCUP, BLOSSOM, and BUTTERFLY.

They hadn't gone very far when
they saw a lady feeding some
ducks.

She was wearing a BONNET,
a BLOUSE fastened at the neck with
a BROOCH, and around her wrist she wore
a BRACELET.

When she saw Paddington she smiled and said, "Would you like some?"

"Thank you very much," said Paddington. He wrote down BAG and BREAD. He then raised his hat politely and said, "Busy Bee Adventure Trails make you hungry."

This is the sort of day out I like, Mr. Gruber!" Paddington announced, as he took a jar of marmalade from his suitcase and began making a sandwich.

"Ahem, Mr. Brown." Mr. Gruber gave a cough. "I think you were really meant to give the bread to the ducks."

Before Paddington had time to reply there was a loud buzzing noise and something landed on his marmalade.

Paddington gave the object a hard stare before adding BEE to his list.

Next, they came upon a man fishing.

"I think you've struck lucky, Mr. Brown," whispered Mr. Gruber.

He waited patiently while Paddington wrote down BOX, followed by BERET, BEARD, BELT, BUCKLE, BOOTS, BUCKET, and BASKET.

"Would you like to have a try?" asked the man. "You can use some of my worms if you'd like."

Paddington thought that was a very good idea, but first he wrote down B for BAIT.

If you're going in for the Busy Bee competition," said the man, "you should watch out. There's a boy following you and I think he's up to no good."

Paddington was about to say "thank you" when he felt a tug on the fishing line. "I think it might be too big to go in my jar, whatever it is!" he exclaimed. "It feels like a W for WHALE."

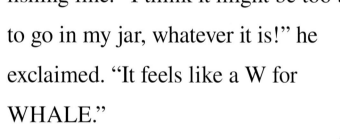

"I'm not sure you'll find any whales this far inland,
Mr. Brown," said Mr. Gruber tactfully.

All the same, to be on the safe side Mr. Gruber tied
some rope around his friend.

"Strike me pink!" said the fisherman. "It's a BICYCLE!" Paddington was most disappointed.

"Never mind," said Mr. Gruber. "At least it's another word for your list."

Shortly afterward they came
upon a stretch of water with
high banks and trees on either
side. Paddington decided to have
a go at riding the bicycle.

But he soon discovered why it
had been thrown away. "I think I'd
better hold the other end, Mr. Gruber,"
he gasped, pointing to the rope still tied around
his waist. "In case I fall in the canal."

Mr. Gruber was about to explain that if he did that there would be nothing for anyone else to hold on to, when he saw the look on Paddington's face.

"Is anything the matter, Mr. Brown?" he asked.

"I think we're being followed by a B for BUSH, Mr. Gruber," hissed Paddington.

"Come back!"
shouted Mr. Gruber,
"whoever you are!"

Meanwhile, Paddington
added BINOCULARS to his list.

While he was writing, a boat went past and one of the passengers had a BABY on her lap. She was feeding him from a BOTTLE. The baby was wearing a BIB and his sister was holding a BALL.

Mr. Gruber sat down by the water while Paddington added up his list.

Altogether, with the BANK and BRAMBLES next to Mr. Gruber, he had forty-one things beginning with the letter B.

Mr. Gruber looked at his watch. "I think it's time we got back, Mr. Brown," he said. "We don't want to be late for the judging."

"Good luck," called the fisherman as they went past.

"We shall be cheering you on," said the lady feeding the ducks.

"Has anyone collected more than forty B's?" called the judge.

"I have!" cried Paddington, waving his piece of paper excitedly. "I've got forty-one."

"So have I!" came a voice from nearby.

Mr. Gruber looked over the boy's shoulder. "This list is exactly the same as young Mr. Brown's," he said sternly. "You must have been copying it—word for word!"

"Oh, dear," said the judge. "We can't have that. I'm afraid
I shall have to stop the contest!"

"It's all right, Mr. Gruber!" called Paddington. "We've
won. I've thought of another B. That gives me forty-two."

"Fancy nearly forgetting the most important item of all," said Mr. Gruber, as they set off on their boat trip. "What made you think of it?"

"I saw my reflection in the water," explained Paddington.

Mr. Gruber nodded. "It's often the hardest of all to see things that are right under your nose," he said.

"It is if you're a B for BEAR," agreed Paddington. "Bears have very long noses."

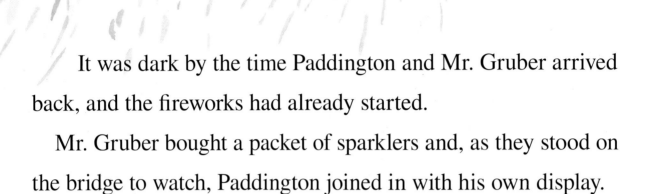

It was dark by the time Paddington and Mr. Gruber arrived back, and the fireworks had already started.

Mr. Gruber bought a packet of sparklers and, as they stood on the bridge to watch, Paddington joined in with his own display.

With his sparkler he waved

Thank you Mr. Gruber for a lovely day out!

In the excitement the only person who noticed was Mr. Gruber himself, but that was really all that mattered.

"If you ask me, Mr. Brown," said Mr. Gruber, as they made their way home, "the nicest B of all is yet to come." "I think I know what that is," said Paddington sleepily. "It's B for BED!"

PADDINGTON
and the Magic Trick

It was Paddington's first birthday
since moving in with the Browns.
Everyone was getting ready
for the party.
Judy hung streamers.
Jonathan blew up balloons.

Paddington could hardly contain
his excitement.

Mrs. Bird baked a special cake

for the big day.

She filled it with marmalade

and covered it with icing.

Paddington wanted a taste.

Mrs. Bird let him lick the spoon.

It was the best birthday cake

he'd ever tasted!

Paddington went to look

at his presents.

He opened his new magic set.

He put on the hat and cape.

Paddington had a great idea!

He would perform at the party.

But first he had to learn

a few magic tricks.

Paddington waved the magic wand.

"Abracadabra!" he said.

He did not see his marmalade jar

drop into the secret drawer.

The trick worked!

Paddington practiced some more.

He couldn't wait to perform

for his guests.

Soon the guests arrived.

Paddington's good friend,

Mr. Gruber, led the way.

Everyone sang "Happy Birthday."
Then Paddington blew out
the candles on his cake.

It was time for the magic show.
Paddington set up
his magic box.

Jonathan and Judy
dimmed the lights.
Everyone was excited
to see Paddington perform.

Paddington put an egg

on the magic box.

He covered it with a scarf.

He said the magic word.

He waved his wand.

The egg had disappeared!

Paddington took a bow.

He tucked his paw
into the secret drawer
to get the egg.

Ta-da! It was . . . a jar.

Paddington was surprised.

How had a jar

ended up where the egg

was supposed to be?

Paddington's guests smiled

and waited for the next trick.

Next Paddington would make

flowers disappear.

But he could not remember

all the steps.

Paddington opened a large door
in the back of the box.

He crawled inside to check
the steps in his magic book.

His guests waited and waited.

Was this the trick?

Finally, Mr. Gruber

knocked on the box.

"Are you okay in there, Mr. Brown?"

Paddington was stuck!

Mr. Brown helped Paddington
out of the box.

"Maybe you could do
another kind of magic trick,"
Mrs. Brown suggested.

Paddington tried a card trick.

Mr. Gruber picked a card.

Paddington tore it
into little pieces.

"This part is tricky,"

said Paddington.

He covered the card with his scarf.

Paddington waved the wand.

"Abracadabra!" he said.

"Oh!" said Mr. Gruber.

"The trick worked!"

He put his hand behind his ear

and pulled out a coin.

Mr. Gruber handed him the coin.

Paddington knew just how

he would spend it.

He would buy their next

morning buns!

PADDINGTON'S
Day Off

One day Paddington went
out for a walk.

He got out his basket on wheels
and put on his coat and hat.

He wanted to see his friend
Mr. Gruber, who owned a shop
in the Portobello Road market.

Mr. Gruber made them some cocoa.

Paddington had some buns to eat.

"It's such a beautiful day,"

Mr. Gruber said.

"Let's take the day off!"

Mr. Gruber closed up the shop.
Paddington hung a sign
on the door.

Paddington and Mr. Gruber
invited Jonathan and Judy
to come along, too.
They packed a lunch.

Paddington brought his suitcase,

a map, and his guidebook.

He also brought his opera glasses.

Mr. Gruber pointed out
lots of things as they passed
by stores and cafés.

Paddington stopped and said hello

to everyone they saw along the way.

Mr. Gruber led them
through a gate into a park.
Paddington was amazed.

There was so much to see and do!

They stopped for lunch by the lake.
Paddington dipped his paws
into the water while he ate
his marmalade sandwich.

At the amusement area,
they played on the slide
and the swings.

Then Mr. Gruber said,

"What's that sound?"

They all stopped to listen.

They heard music playing.

They walked farther into the park
and found a little bandstand.
A band was playing!

Mr. Gruber found some empty chairs.

They all sat down.

Mr. Gruber read the program.

"They are playing

a famous Surprise Symphony!"

Paddington loved surprises.

He wondered what

the surprise would be.

Paddington decided to ask
the band about the surprise.

He walked around the bandstand.

There was a door marked "Private."

It opened easily.

Inside, Paddington looked around.

It was dark and dusty and gloomy.

The door closed behind him.

Paddington pushed on the door.

It wouldn't open!

Paddington found an old broom.

He pounded on the ceiling.

Mr. Gruber wondered
where Paddington had gone.
The music was playing.
It didn't sound right.

PRIVATE

Bump, bump, bump!
The sound was coming
from under the stage.

Bump, BUMP, BUMP!

The conductor jumped.

The sound was coming

from under his feet.

The conductor reached down
and opened a door in the stage.

"Oh!" he exclaimed.

"It's a bear!"

The conductor helped Paddington
climb onto the stage.
"Would you like to finish
the Surprise Symphony?" he asked.
He handed Paddington his baton.

Paddington waved the baton
in the air and then took his bow.
Everyone clapped and cheered.
It was a surprising end
to a most enjoyable day off!

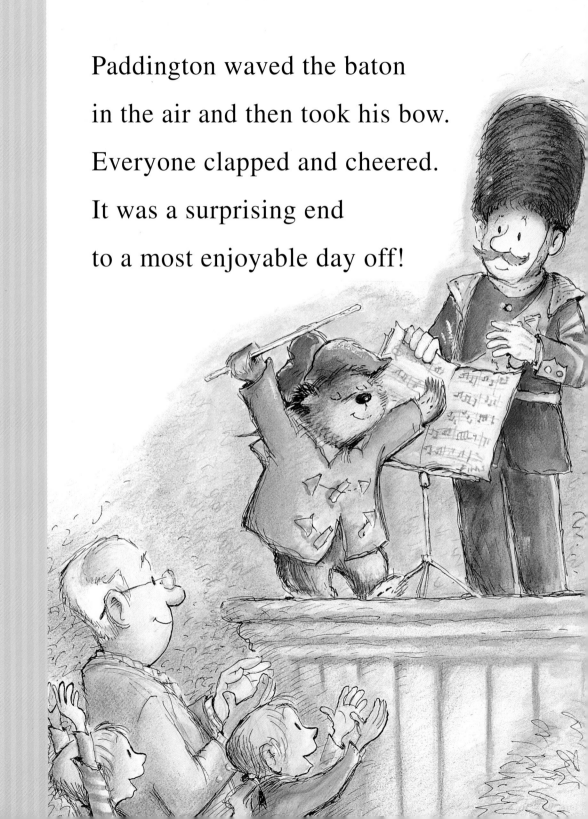

PADDINGTON

in the Garden

ne morning Paddington went out into the garden and began making a list of all the nice things he could think of about being a bear and living with the Browns.

He had a room of his own and a warm bed to sleep in. And he had marmalade for breakfast *every* morning. In Darkest Peru he had only been allowed to have it on Sundays.

The list was soon so long he had nearly run out of paper before he realized he had left out one of the nicest things of all . . .

. . . the garden itself!

Paddington liked the Browns' garden. Apart from the occasional noise from a nearby building site, it was so quiet and peaceful it didn't seem like being in London at all.

But nice gardens don't just happen. They usually require a lot of hard work, and the one at number thirty-two Windsor Gardens was no exception. Mr. Brown had to mow the lawn twice a week, and Mrs. Brown was kept busy weeding the flower beds. There was always something to do. Even Mrs. Bird lent a hand whenever she had a spare moment.

103

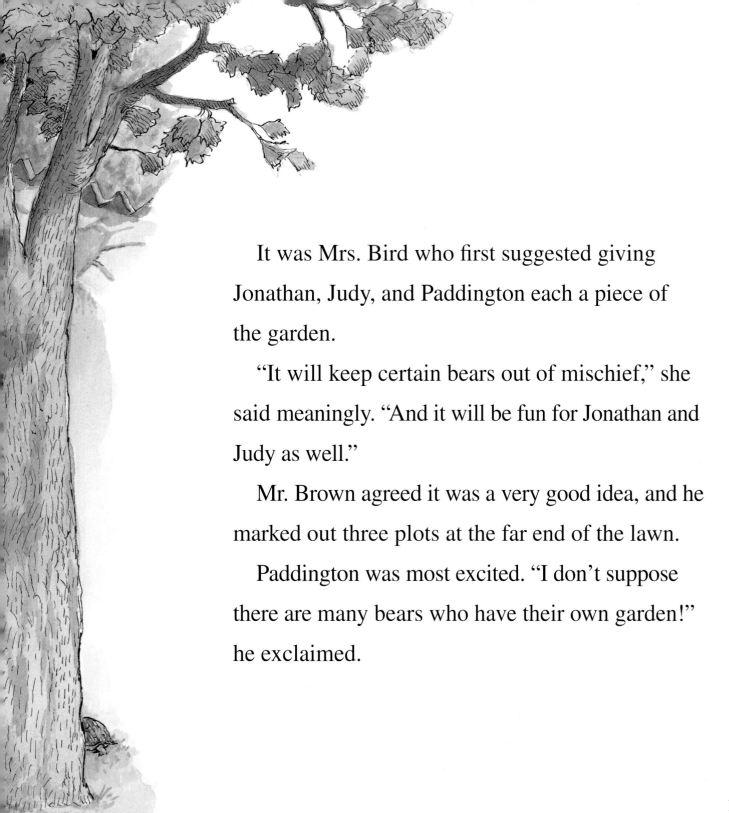

It was Mrs. Bird who first suggested giving Jonathan, Judy, and Paddington each a piece of the garden.

"It will keep certain bears out of mischief," she said meaningly. "And it will be fun for Jonathan and Judy as well."

Mr. Brown agreed it was a very good idea, and he marked out three plots at the far end of the lawn.

Paddington was most excited. "I don't suppose there are many bears who have their own garden!" he exclaimed.

Early the next morning all three set to work.

Judy decided to make a flower bed and Jonathan
had his eye on some old paving stones.

Paddington didn't know what
to do. In the past he had often
found that gardening was much
harder than it looked, especially
when you only had paws.

In the end, armed with a jar of Mrs. Bird's
homemade marmalade, he borrowed Mr. Brown's
wheelbarrow and set off to look for ideas.

His first stop was a stall in the market, where he bought a book called *How to Plan Your Garden* by Lionel Trug.

It came complete with a large packet of assorted seeds, and if the picture on the front cover was anything to go by, it was no wonder Mr. Trug looked happy, for he seemed to do most of his planning while lying in a hammock. By the end of the book, without lifting a finger, he was surrounded by blooms.

Paddington decided it was a very good value indeed—especially when the owner of the stall gave him two pence change.

Mr. Trug's book was full of useful
hints and tips.

The first one suggested that before starting
work it was a good idea to close your eyes
and try to picture what the garden
would look like when it was finished.

Having walked into a lamppost by mistake,
Paddington decided to read another page or two, and
there he found a much better idea. Mr. Trug advised
standing back and looking at the site from a
safe distance, preferably somewhere
high up.

Paddington knew just the spot.

By the time Paddington reached the building site near the Browns' house it was the middle of the morning, and the men were all on their tea break.

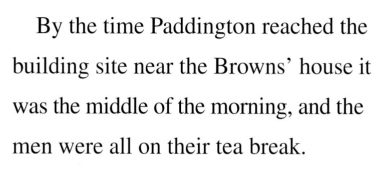

Placing his jar of marmalade on a wooden platform for safekeeping, he sat on a pile of bricks for a rest while he considered the matter.

There was no one about. . . .

And there was a ladder nearby. . . .

Mr. Trug was quite right. The Browns'
garden did look very different from high
up. But before he had time to get his breath
back, Paddington heard the sound of an
engine starting up. He peered through a
gap in the boards. As he did so his eyes
nearly popped out.

On the ground just below him, a man
was emptying a load of concrete on the
very spot where he had left his jar of marmalade!

Paddington scrambled back down the ladder as fast as
his legs would carry him, reaching the bottom just as the
foreman came around a corner.

"Is anything wrong?" asked the man. "You look upset."

"My jar's been buried!" exclaimed Paddington hotly, pointing to the pile of concrete. "It had some of Mrs. Bird's best golden chunks in it, too!"

"I won't ask how your jar got there," said the foreman, turning to Paddington as his men set to work clearing the concrete into small piles, "*or what you were doing up the ladder.*"

"I'm glad of that," said Paddington, politely raising his hat.

Suddenly there was a whirring
sound from somewhere overhead, and
to Paddington's surprise the platform
landed at his feet. "My marmalade!"
he exclaimed thankfully.

"Your *marmalade*?" repeated the foreman, staring at the jar. "Did you say marmalade?"

"That's right," said Paddington.

"I put it there ready for my elevenses. It must have been taken up by mistake. Now the top's come off!"

It was the foreman's turn to look as though he could hardly believe his eyes.

"That's special quick-drying cement!" he wailed. "It's probably rock-hard already—ruined by a bear's marmalade! No one will give me tuppence for it now!"

"I will," said Paddington eagerly. "I've had an idea!"

Paddington was busy for the rest of the week.

When the builders saw the rock garden he had made, they were most impressed, and the foreman even gave him some plants to finish it off until his seeds started to grow.

"It's National Garden Day on Saturday," he said. "There are some very famous people judging it. I'll spread the word around. You never know your luck."

The foreman was as good as his word, and on Saturday half the neighborhood turned up at number thirty-two Windsor Gardens to see the judges arrive.

Paddington nearly fell over backwards with surprise when he discovered that no less a person than Mr. Lionel Trug himself was leading the procession.

"It's very good of you to get out of your hammock, Mr. Trug!" he exclaimed.

"Er . . . not at all," said Lionel Trug. "My pleasure. I must say, I love your orange stones. Where *did* you find them?"

"I didn't," said Paddington. "I think they found me. Thanks to the builders."

"Congratulations!" said Mr. Trug as he handed Paddington a gold star. "It's good to see a young bear taking up gardening. I hope you will be the first of many."

"Who would have believed it?" said Mr. Brown as the last of the crowd departed.

"You must write and tell Aunt Lucy all about it," said Mrs. Bird. "They'll be very excited in the Home for Retired Bears when they hear the news."

Paddington thought that was a good idea, but he had something to do first.

He wanted to add one more important item to his list of all the nice things there were about being a bear and living with the Browns:

HAVING MY OWN ROCK GARDEN!

Then he signed his name and added his special paw print . . . just to show it was genuine.

PADDINGTON
at the Circus

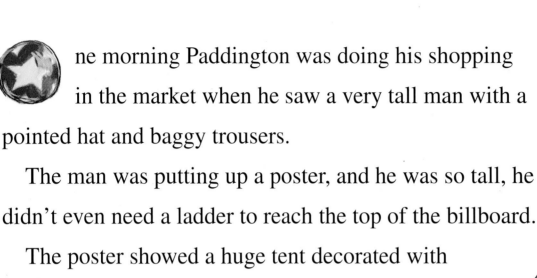

ne morning Paddington was doing his shopping in the market when he saw a very tall man with a pointed hat and baggy trousers.

The man was putting up a poster, and he was so tall, he didn't even need a ladder to reach the top of the billboard.

The poster showed a huge tent decorated with colored lights, and across the middle were the words SEE THE WORLD'S GREATEST CIRCUS. ONE NIGHT ONLY.

Paddington rubbed his eyes several times in order to make sure he wasn't dreaming.

Paddington hurried back home to tell the others
what he had seen.

"The world's greatest circus?" repeated Jonathan,
giving his sister a wink. "Are you sure?"

"It's for one night only!"
exclaimed Paddington.

"Don't worry," said Judy.
"You won't miss it."

"Dad's got tickets for the front
row," added Jonathan. "Mrs. Bird's
coming, too."

Paddington had never been to
a circus before, and he was very
excited at the thought. "I hope it gets
dark early," he said. "Then we can
see the lights."

Paddington's wish came true. Seen from the outside, with all the colored lights twinkling against the night sky, the circus really did have a magical air.

"Hurry! Hurry! Have your tickets ready!" called a voice. "The show's about to begin!"

"It's the man I saw this morning," whispered Paddington. "The very tall one I was telling you about."

"That's one of the clowns," said Judy.

"He isn't really that tall . . . ," began Jonathan. But Paddington couldn't wait. He could hear a band playing, and he was already hurrying on ahead.

But if the outside of the tent had seemed exciting, it was nothing compared to the inside.

There was a lovely smell of sawdust, and in among the jugglers and the acrobats there was even a girl selling ice cream.

Mr. Brown pointed to a man in the middle of the ring. He was wearing a top hat.

"That's the ringmaster," he explained. "He's in charge of everything."

"I expect you could keep a lot of marmalade sandwiches under a hat like that," said Paddington enviously. "I think I would like to be a ringmaster one day."

Just then the tall clown entered the ring. He was clutching a long pole that had a bucket balanced on the end of it. When he saw Paddington waving, he came across to greet him.

"Watch out!" cried Jonathan as the clown leaned over to shake Paddington's paw.

Paddington jumped up in alarm. But he wasn't quick enough. Before he had time to escape, the bucket had fallen off the end of the pole.

Luckily, it was tied on with string and it was empty, so Paddington didn't get wet.

"Clowns are full of tricks," said Judy.

"I'm glad I was wearing my duffle coat all the same," said Paddington. "Someone might have put water in the bucket by mistake."

"I'm told ice cream is very good for young bears if they've had a shock," said Mr. Brown.

He ordered six large cones, then they all sat back to enjoy the show.

"I feel better already, Mr. Brown," said Paddington gratefully.

Paddington had hardly started on his ice cream when he had yet another shock.

Glancing up toward the roof of the tent, he saw a man hanging from a rope.

Jonathan looked at his program. "That must be one of the Popular Prices," he said. "They're trapeze artists."

"Don't worry!" called Paddington. "I'm coming. Bears are good at climbing."

Before the others could stop him, Paddington
was halfway up the nearest tent pole.

Climbing the pole and carrying an ice cream
at the same time wasn't easy, and the
audience gave a round of applause when
he reached the safety of a small
platform near the top.

Paddington was about to take a bow when, to his
surprise, he saw a man coming toward him on a bicycle.
"I don't think you're supposed to bring your bicycle
up here, Mr. Price!" he exclaimed.

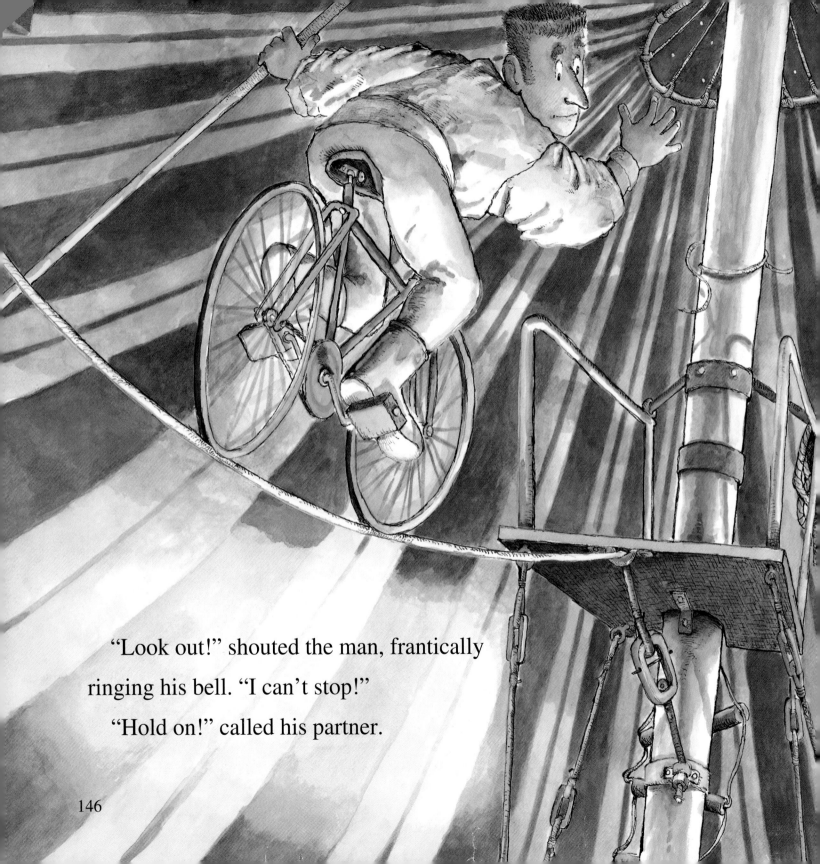

"Look out!" shouted the man, frantically ringing his bell. "I can't stop!"

"Hold on!" called his partner.

146

In the confusion, Paddington didn't know which to
do first, so he grabbed hold of a nearby bar.

It came away in his paw, and before he knew what
was happening, he felt himself flying through the air.

The audience thought Paddington was part of the act, and they clapped louder than ever.

Then a gasp went up as he missed the platform on the other side of the tent and began swinging backward and forward in midair.

"Oh dear!" said Mrs. Brown. "Whatever will he do now?"

"I shouldn't worry," said Mrs. Bird. "Bears usually land on their feet."

But even Mrs. Bird went quiet as Paddington's swings got slower and slower, until finally he ended up hanging over the middle of the ring.

"Don't let go!" shouted the ringmaster. "Whatever you do—don't let go!"

"I'm not going to!" cried Paddington.

He tried to raise his hat, but he was still holding the ice cream cone in his other paw.

A look of horror came over the ringmaster's face as something soft and white landed with a *squelch* on his beautifully clean top hat.

"Help!" cried Paddington. "I've changed my mind. I can't hold on much longer."

Everybody in the audience began making suggestions, but in the end it was the clown who came to the rescue.

Balancing his bucket on the end of the pole, he stretched up as high as he could so Paddington could climb into it.

"I hope the string doesn't break," said Mrs. Bird. "That bear had a very large lunch."

"If the clown stretches any more," said Judy, "his trousers will fall down."

Sure enough they did, and the cheers changed
to laughter as Paddington was lowered to safety.

"Funniest act I've seen in years!" shouted a man near the Browns. "More! More!"

Paddington gave the man a hard stare. "I don't think I want to do any more," he announced. "In fact, I don't think I want to go on a trapeze ever again. I shall just sit and watch from now on."

Then he caught sight of the clown's stilts. "It's no wonder you look so tall!" he exclaimed.

Paddington didn't think anything more *could* happen to him, but at the end of the evening the ringmaster presented him with another ice cream and insisted he take part in the Grand Parade.

"After all," he said, "you *were* the star of the show.

"It's a pity we are moving on," he added, turning to the Browns. "It isn't every evening we have a daring young bear on the flying trapeze."

"If you ask me," said Mrs. Bird wisely, "it's a good thing you don't. Otherwise there's no knowing where you would end up."

Later that evening, when the Browns said good night to Paddington, they found him standing on the box seat by his bedroom window. He had a faraway look in his eyes.

"I was taking a last look at the circus before it goes on its way," he explained.

"Do you still want to be a ringmaster one day?" asked Judy.

Paddington climbed into bed and tested his sheets carefully to make sure he was safely tucked in before answering. Then he lay back.

"I think perhaps I would sooner be a clown," he said dreamily. "It must be nice to be so tall. You can always see what's going on in the world without having to stand on anything."

PADDINGTON'S
Prize Picture

One morning, Mrs. Brown
sent Paddington to the market
to buy some oranges.

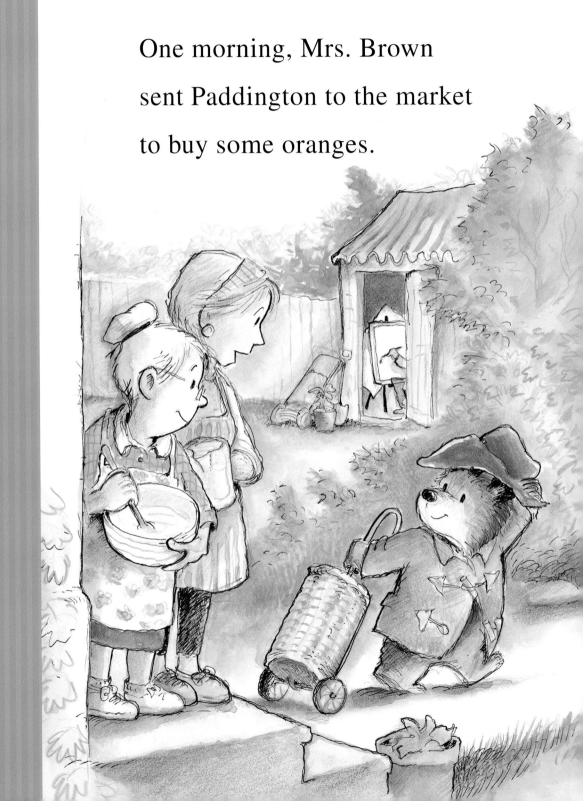

Paddington was well-known

in the market.

The traders always saved

their best fruit for him.

And he always thanked them for it!

When he was done shopping,
Paddington visited
his friend Mr. Gruber.

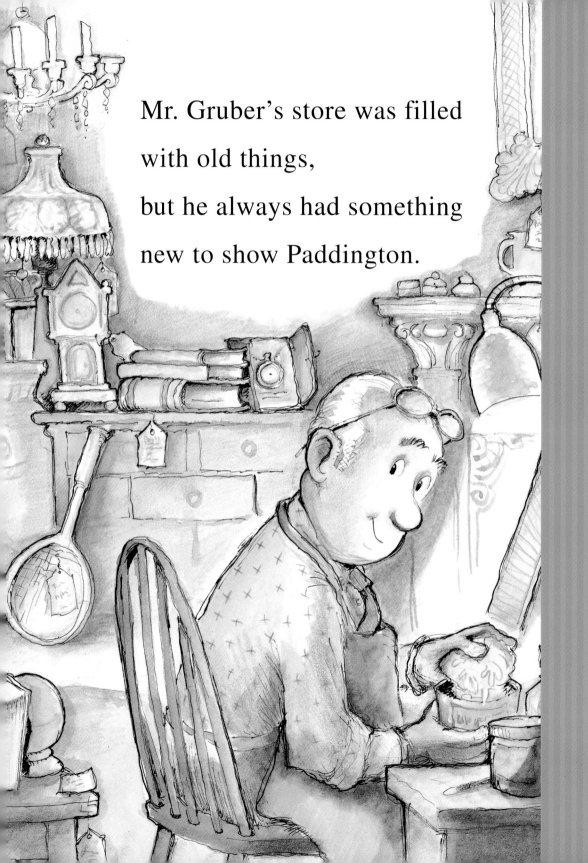

Mr. Gruber's store was filled
with old things,
but he always had something
new to show Paddington.

Mr. Gruber was very busy.

He was washing a painting.

On one half Paddington saw
a picture of a boat.

On the other half Paddington saw
what looked like a hat.

"Just you wait," said Mr. Gruber.

"There's more to come."

"I've never seen a picture

like this before," said Paddington.

"That's because one picture

is hidden under another,"

Mr. Gruber said.

Paddington had a great idea.

He hurried home as fast
as his legs would carry him.

169

Paddington looked for the picture

Mr. Brown had been painting.

He wondered if this one had

another picture under it, too.

Paddington began to clean.

The boats and blue sky disappeared,

but there was nothing underneath.

The beautiful picture
was now a stormy sea.
Paddington decided
to fix it.

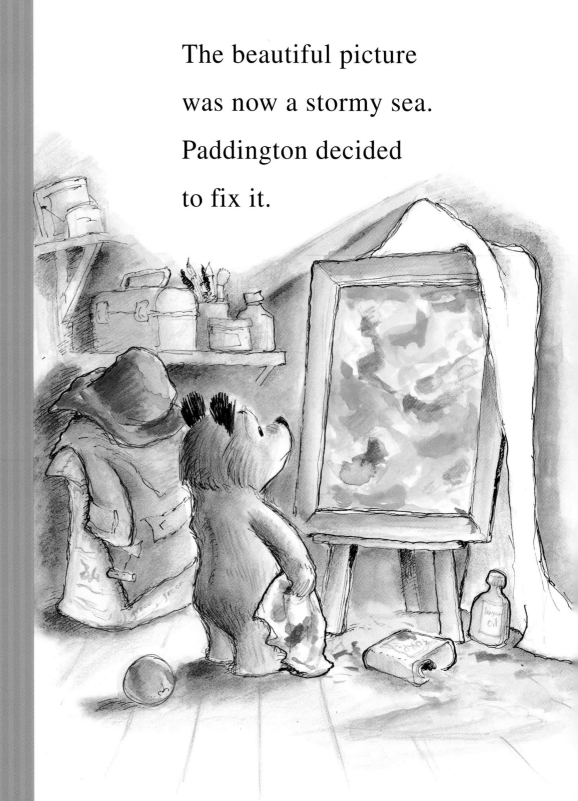

He found some brushes
and an old box of paints.

Then Paddington set to work.

He started to paint

the boats and the lake.

He carefully filled in

the spots he had cleaned.

Paddington stepped back

to look at his work.

There was no lake.

There were no boats.

He reached for the paints

and began again.

At dinner that evening,
Paddington was covered
in orange spots.

"I hope you're not getting sick,"
said Mrs. Brown.
She sent him to bed early
just in case.

The next morning,
everyone was happy
to see that Paddington's
spots were gone.

"I have news," said Mr. Brown.

"I have entered a painting contest.

You must all come to the show."

The art show began.
The judges looked
at all the paintings.

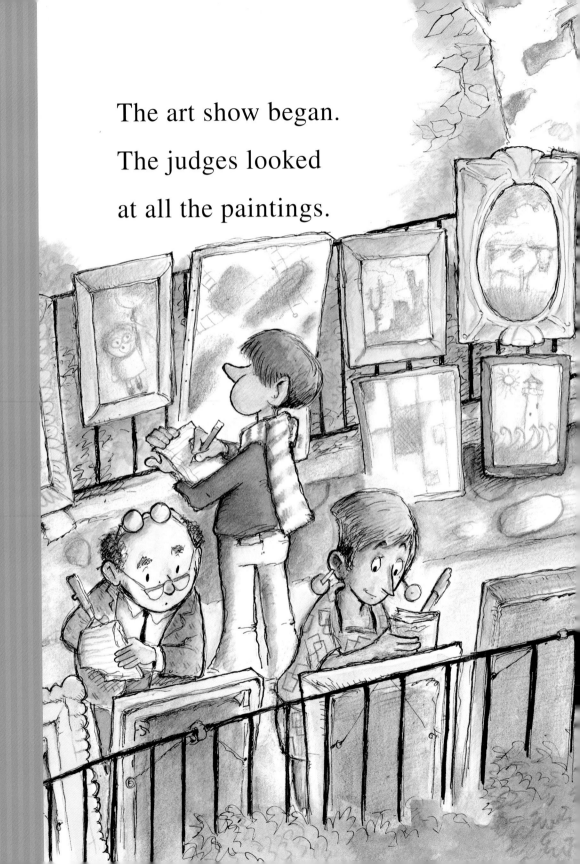

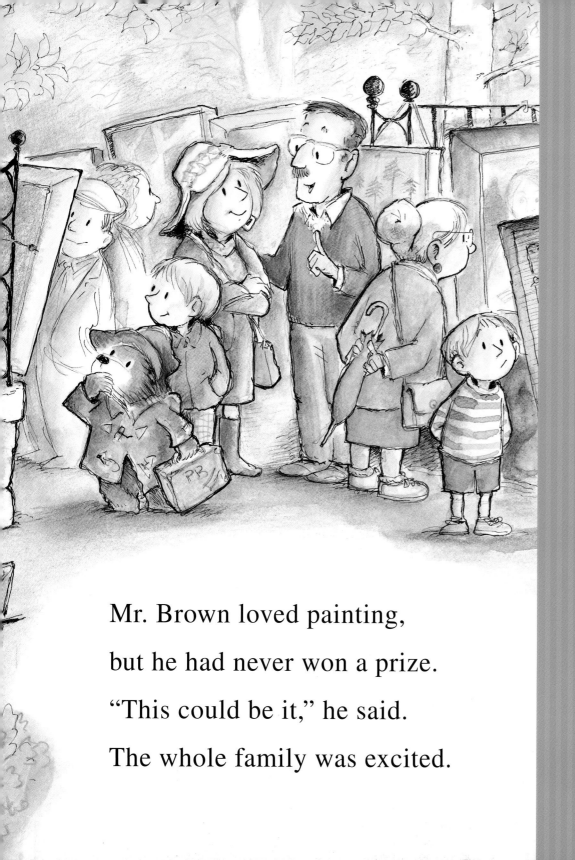

Mr. Brown loved painting,

but he had never won a prize.

"This could be it," he said.

The whole family was excited.

The judges announced the winner.

It was Mr. Brown!

But Mr. Brown looked confused.

"This is not my painting!"

said Mr. Brown.

"There must be some mistake."

Paddington's painting
on Mr. Brown's canvas
won first prize!

The judges showed Mr. Brown

his name written on the back.

Mr. Brown accepted his prize. "I think I will donate my prize to the Home for Retired Bears in Peru," he said.

Paddington beamed.

"My aunt Lucy will be pleased.

She likes happy endings."

"Don't we all," said Mrs. Bird.

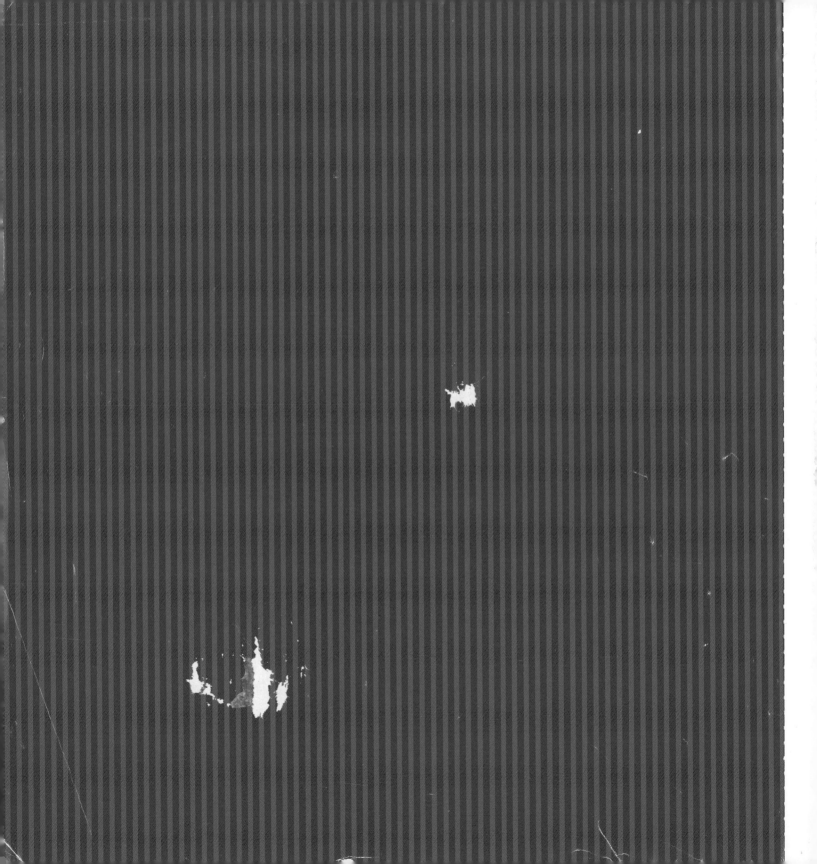